LOVE ME DIRTY

LOVE ME DIRTY

LILIAN T. JAMES

Crystal Pages Publishing is an imprint of
Aleron Books LLC

First printing edition 2022

Cover Design : Murphy Rae
Editor : Allusion Publishing
Chapter Header Designs : Etheric Tales & Edits

ISBN-13: 978-1-7378899-7-7

To all of you who have ever been made to feel 'less than' or worthless. Take back your power. It looks fucking gorgeous on you.

Author's Note

Please be aware, this is a short, character-driven, insta-lust novella. Content includes detailed sexual scenes, including consensual degradation, spit play, and anal play. If you're looking for a sweet, slowburn romance with a detailed plot, this isn't it.

Although both can be read as standalones, I do recommend you read *Meet Me Halfway* prior to *Love Me Dirty* to have more fun and catch small details.

Chapter 1

Bartender

I STARED AT my hands, resting against two wet, naked breasts, wondering if it was possible to flatten one with just my hand.

I pulled my arm back and smacked the edge of my fist against the left one, analyzing how it responded. It didn't seem to do a whole lot. Huh. Maybe I just needed to smack it harder.

I'd just raised my hand again when a feminine voice spoke behind me, pulling me out of my angry—seemingly ineffective—musings.

"What on Earth are you doing?"

"Working. Something you're obviously not doing," I said, not bothering to turn around.

"Jackass. You do realize the chicken's already dead, right?"

"How the fuck should I know? Do I look like a goddamn cook to you?" I grumbled, slapping the slimy chicken breast again. I didn't even eat meat; I shouldn't have to fucking prepare it.

"I suppose that answers my next question of how you're doing today."

I made drinks. Freaking bomb-ass drinks, to be honest. I mixed and poured, and sometimes I threw in a few bottle flips when I wanted extra tips or a specific patron's attention.

I was a quiet, patient ear for lonely, middle-aged customers, and a cheerleader for the young drunk ones. Hell, I even offered advice to any who seemed to need it, knowing full well not a word would be remembered or used.

And when I was in a good mood, I'd give people free baskets of fries and sneak maraschino cherries to quiet kids when their parents weren't looking.

I. Didn't. Fucking. Cook. At least, not here in poultry hell.

Sensing her stare and realizing she wasn't going to leave until I acknowledged her, I turned toward my unwanted company. Unwanted only because Madison Hartland was one of the most observant people I'd ever met.

And as one of my closest friends, the woman saw through my swagger as easily as if I were see-through—even when I didn't want her to.

She stood just on the other side of the hot counter, sporting a messy mane of curls barely contained in a clip, and the all-knowing look only a mother could possess.

"I'm not in the mood for pointless banter tonight, Curly. I'm busy," I glanced over my shoulder at the slabs of raw chicken carcass, "tenderizing meat."

She dipped her head forward, holding both hands up in surrender. "All right, Nate, I can take a hint. I'll leave you be. But just so you know, the tool next to you is a meat mallet. Maybe give it a try when you're done with your hissy fit."

She grabbed her table's plates from the counter, stacking an assembly line of sodium and preservatives down her arm.

"Let me know if you want to stay after work and chat it out," she added, giving me one last scrutinizing look, before scurrying out.

Tipping my head back, I raised my hands in a silent plea to a God I didn't believe in, and released a long, drawn-out curse.

Frustrated would be an understatement. I was beyond frustrated. With my boss, with this job, and with my inability to grow a pair and quit so I could focus on the work that actually paid my bills.

I shouldn't have lashed out at Madison just because I

was cranky as shit. She was the most caring person I'd ever met, and she'd just been trying to check up on me. I could've been honest without being a jerk.

Maybe next time she came around I'd make it up to her with a teasing remark about her boyfriend, Garrett, and his overbearing tendencies. Those always worked. The memory of him verbally pissing on me to stake his claim on her always brought a smile to her face.

I sighed, turning back toward the counter, and grabbed the weird, spiky hammer she'd pointed out. I'd wondered what it was for.

Lifting it, I slammed it onto the meat with more force than was necessary, imagining my boss's face. It was surprisingly therapeutic.

He'd called me last night—my last night off this week—asking me to come in early today. I'd agreed, not thinking much about it. I'd figured the woman who worked the day shift had an appointment or something to get to. No biggie.

What the shithead failed to mention during the call was that he wanted me to come in early to cover a few hours for a *cook* who was arriving late.

Given the way my boss had fled to his office when I arrived, it was safe to assume he'd misled me on purpose and knew I'd be pissed.

Between my physical appearance and the fact that he was several years younger than me, it didn't surprise me he'd run. I'd call him a pussy, but I've felt the tight clench of many, and there was nothing weak about that. The little shit was more like a ball sack that was too scared to drop.

He assumed the same thing everyone else did who met me, that I was trouble with a capital T. Likely mixed up with drugs or living under a fake identity after escaping prison. Madison had been the only person here who'd bothered to get to know me.

But none of that mattered when I was still stuck coming into this goddamn kitchen. No matter how much I wanted to tell my boss to fuck off, I'd given my word and agreed to come in, and I didn't break my word. I was going to do the stupid job whether I wanted to or not.

Grumbling, I continued working my way through the food prep, cursing up a storm while simultaneously telling myself to stop being a whiney shit over it.

If Madison could work sixty hours a week at jobs she hated, I could handle throwing around some slimy meat for a few hours before my normal shift started.

I glanced at the clock to see how much longer I had and nearly chucked the hammer thing across the room when it showed another hour. It was going to be a long ass night.

Here's to hoping at least something fun happened to make up for it. Maybe Garrett would pop in, and I'd give Madison a nice big hug just to see steam pour out of his ears.

I might end the night dead and stuffed in a porta-john, but it'd sure be an entertaining fucking way to go.

CHAPTER 2

Lacey

YOU KNOW THAT feeling you get when you're in the middle of an interview, and your nose suddenly starts running? Or when you're driving on an interstate with a case of liquid butt horror, and the next rest stop is still sixty-six miles away?

How about when you do something you weren't supposed to do, and your phone chimes with the proof, only for your girlfriend to whip her arm out and snatch it up before you do?

That's how I felt walking into the restaurant alone.

My heart was a hammer in my chest, my stomach

nothing but a swirl of bile, and my veins full of ice. I'd finally done it. It'd been messy and ugly as hell, but I'd left Derek in the dust and was ready for the next stage of my life.

I should've been celebrating in my pajamas with a glass of red wine, dancing to my favorite playlist and singing at the top of my lungs.

But instead, I was drowning in anxiety and walking into a random restaurant I just happened to pass when I realized I couldn't bear to go home alone. Not without some liquid courage at least. I needed to ease into my first night as an unwanted single woman before the reality of it raw-dogged me in the ass.

"Just one or are you meeting someone?"

I tore my gaze from the alcohol-filled bar I'd been staring at, to look at the girl working the hostess stand. She had the widest smile I'd ever seen, but the moment we locked eyes, it fell, and she looked ten seconds away from high-tailing it from the lobby.

Great, the night had only just started, and I'd already terrified an unsuspecting teenager because I couldn't get my angry, bitch face under control. Lovely.

Mentally punching myself, I wiped the unintentional glare off my face, and waved a hand toward the bar. "It's just me tonight. Is it cool if I sit at the bar?"

She set her little stack of menus down, releasing a sigh of relief I probably wasn't meant to hear. "Yes, ma'am, that's fine."

Ma'am. Ugh. I'd lived on the east coast for most of my adult life, but I still couldn't get used to the way everyone here always wanted to call me "ma'am." Like I was a fifty-year-old woman sporting straight bangs and a cardigan, rather than the pink-haired, almost thirty-year-old I was.

No. Not almost thirty. Twenty-nine. Who cared that my birthday was in a few weeks? I was only twenty-nine, and I was sticking to that, damnit.

Dodging a waitress who turned too quickly with an armful of plates, I power-walked my ass to the bar in record time. It was fuller than I would've expected for a Sunday night, but there was a stool right on the end that called my name with flying banners.

I slid onto it, propping my heeled feet on the footrest, and wiggled out of my jacket. This was what I needed before going home to crash on the couch. Just an hour to sit back, sip a drink or two, and flaunt the face of makeup I'd painstakingly put on.

Because Lord knew, I had zero desire to sleep on a mattress that Derek and I had shared. Not after today. I'd rather curl up on a fucking life-size spider web before I ever slept there again.

Ugh. I needed that drink, *now*. I glanced around for the bartender twice before my eyes finally zeroed in on a man standing on the other side of the bar. Dressed in a black shirt and dark jeans, leaning over the counter as he was, I'd missed him at first.

But there was no missing him now.

Looking to be around twenty-five, he was maybe a few inches taller than I was when I wore heels, but his presence seemed to command the room like he owned the entire building.

His midnight black hair was shaved close to his head on the sides, but long and slicked back on top, and his green eyes were vivid, even from five seats down.

I chewed my lip, watching the way his throat moved as he laughed at something an older gentleman said. He nodded in agreement with whatever their conversation was and began shoving his sleeves up, revealing a drool-worthy array of tattoos on both arms.

Holy hell.

He wasn't what I would call muscular, but he wasn't thin either, and the middle ground in which his body resided was absolute perfection. Toned but not thick. Dangerous but not serial killer-y.

Feeling almost hypnotized, I watched him dip his hands into a small sink and pull out a glass, running his long fingers just inside the dripping rim in a way that had me crossing my legs and squeezing.

The mind-numbing arousal that slammed into me had me swallowing hard. What the *hell?*

I had no problem noticing hot guys—seeing, interacting, and flirting with them was literally part of my job description—but I'd never had such an instant knee-jerk reaction before.

I'd never found myself immediately imagining what

it'd be like to invite a man home after only one look. And I'd definitely never stared longingly at his lips, wondering what they might feel like against mine. Until now.

Granted, I hadn't exactly been in the market to take a man home in a while, but still. In that moment, I couldn't help but picture exactly that.

Especially when he turned my way, and his eyes snapped to mine like he'd been aware of me the entire time. His lips curved into a smile I was sure was just meant to say, "Hello," but effectively disintegrated my panties.

Fuck.

He snatched a towel from next to the sink and rubbed it over his hands, focusing on the crevices between each individual finger as he made his way toward me.

"You look like you could use a drink."

Ouch. Okay, so he obviously wasn't on the same page as me. Typical. I huffed out a breath. "Is that your signature bartender line, or are you genuinely telling me I look like shit?"

A single, dark brow raised up his forehead, and his smile changed for a moment, turning near devilish before dropping back into an easy grin.

"You've been sporting a frown this entire time, and chose the farthest chair from any other human being. So, let's call it a bartender's intuition."

He winked, and it instantly had my feathers ruffled. What an arrogant asshat. I sucked on my front teeth and said, "Been aware of me the entire time I've sat here, have you?"

Still gripping the towel, he placed both hands on the bar, leaning against it until his face was only a foot away from mine. "Lacey, I've been aware of you since the second you walked through that door."

I wasn't sure what made me angrier. The fact that I'd been attracted to him while he apparently thought I was someone else, or that my body responded to the husky tone of his voice anyway.

CHAPTER 3

Bartender

ON A DYING, polluted rock full of selfish, rotten humans, she was a fucking jewel.

Wearing a maroon blouse tucked into a black, mid-thigh skirt with a leather jacket and heels, she stood out like a diamond tucked amongst ash.

No, not even that was accurate. Diamonds were far too common. With her vibrant pink hair delicately curled to frame her face, and smokey eye makeup that made her blue eyes pop, she was more like an uncut ruby. Rare and desirable.

I wasn't typically drawn to someone by looks alone. I

experienced physical attraction and often joked with Madison about sexy customers, but the truth was that looks weren't that important to me.

I'd taken people home of all identities, shades, shapes, and sizes. And in every case, it was their personalities, their humor, and their viewpoint on life that drew me in and sent blood rushing south.

But when she'd walked in, and I watched her converse with our hostess, I was instantly hooked. With her tight expression and hands resting on a set of hips that flared out over thick, luscious legs, I couldn't help but wonder if maybe I'd just never met the right person.

Because without knowing a single thing about her, I wanted her. To the point that when she gestured toward the bar and began making her way over, I had to pull a random customer into a conversation to keep from blatantly ogling her.

"Not sure what kind of pick-up line that's supposed to be, but my name's not Lacey," she snapped, scowling.

Her misunderstanding of the nickname I'd given her brought a smile to my face, which quickly turned into a laugh when her scowl only deepened.

The expression somehow made her even sexier, and the demon in me that only came out during rough, dirty sex raised his head and licked his lips. I fucking loved a woman who wasn't scared to be blunt.

"Not trying to pick you up at all. I serve a lot of people," I said, extending my arm toward the customers adorning the other stools. "Sometimes all at once."

I winked. "I don't make a habit of asking for and memorizing everyone's names, so the only way to keep you all separate in the computer is if I give you nicknames."

I tipped my head back, allowing my eyes to look up and down her frame. "Calling you Pink Patty or Glaring Gloria didn't seem to fit, so I went with your shirt."

She glanced down at the intricate lace adorning her blouse and grimaced. "Sorry, guess I'm a little aggressive tonight."

The comment, and the truth I heard behind it, irked me. "Why the hell are you sorry? It's not a negative trait to speak your mind when you feel disrespected."

She straightened, eyebrows nearly hitting her hairline as she turned her head and cupped a hand around one ear. "Do you hear that?"

I tossed the rag I'd been pointlessly carrying around and pressed my lips together. Giving a quick shake of my head, I asked, "Hear what?"

"The cries of outraged men everywhere shouting their disagreement with you. You don't hear it? It's quite loud."

The laugh that burst out of me was sudden, to the point of being almost painful, and caused the people sitting nearest us to look over.

When I'd finally mastered myself, I went to grab a new, clean rag for the sole purpose of busying my hands. But as I turned, I caught Madison's gaze from across the room.

Hands full of dishes, she darted her eyes over to Lacey

before coming back to me. I smirked, and she just shook her head, rolling her eyes to the ceiling. She knew me well enough to know when I was in all-out-player mode.

Because win or lose, when I wanted something—or some*one*—I gave it my all to make it happen. And right now, what I wanted, was to take Lacey home. Fuck, did I want to.

I knew she was interested. I'd practically felt the heat of her stare when she'd first sat down, but that didn't mean she was free, or willing, to act on it.

So, I planned to do what I did best. I'd make her a drink, offer her my ear, and make it my goal to get her to laugh. If I got lucky enough to end the night with her grinding her cunt on my face, even better.

"So, tell me, Miss Lace, are you celebrating or wallowing tonight? Because that will determine what drink you'll have."

Her blue eyes narrowed. "Am I not allowed to choose what I want?"

"My bar, my rules." Technically, it wasn't my bar, but as long as I was the one standing behind it, making the drinks, it might as well be.

A spark lit up those gorgeous eyes, and the sight did something to my middle that it shouldn't have. Something that I was choosing to ignore and shove deep down.

She wet her lips. "So, as long as I'm here, you get to choose what goes down my throat?"

The smooth, sweet sound of her voice, mixed with her

question and the challenge in her stare was all it took to have me hard as fuck and ready to go.

"I think, Miss Lace," I said, stopping directly in front of her, "that you would quite like what I put there."

CHAPTER 4

Bartender

SHE SEEMED AT a loss for words. Point one for me. I smirked, shoving back to snatch the order ticket that had just printed near my computer.

Just a beer for table three. Easy enough. I grabbed a frosted mug and stepped over to the tap—which was thankfully close by—and took pity on her. "So, what is it, Lacey? What's your story?"

She cringed, tracing her nails across the grain of the bar. "I broke up with my boyfriend this evening after we had a public fight in the middle of my job."

I looked up, not needing to watch what I was doing to

get that perfect foam-to-liquid ratio. "I want to respond encouragingly, but I'm not sure of the context. However, I feel like any reason to end a relationship is a valid one, so good for you."

She didn't look away from the invisible swirls she was making on the bar. I set the mug on the order mat to be picked up and waited while she worked through her answer.

"It was partly my fault. I'd lied about what I did at my job because I knew he wouldn't approve. He found out today and confronted me about it. It didn't go well, and he said a lot of nasty things I couldn't forgive."

Ah, hell. Just another reason I didn't envy anyone in a relationship. Why be with someone you felt the need to hide things from? And on the other side, why be with someone you had no problem disrespecting? I didn't understand it at all.

Part of me—okay, a large part of me—wanted to ask what she did for a living that she felt the need to lie about. However, one of my top rules I tried to stick to was never delving into someone's personal life they didn't willingly share, and she'd clearly left that detail out for a reason.

"Half happy, half miserable, got it." Tequila it was.

"So, tell me," I continued, grabbing the liquor and some juice off the shelf behind me and getting to work, "what made you want to stop *here* of all places to wallow in celebration for your newly single status?"

Out of the corner of my eye I saw Madison handing out food to a few of my customers for me. I mouthed a quick "thank you," and she smiled, giving me a thumbs up. Bless that woman, she was the best fucking wingman.

"I ended up leaving work early and was driving around aimlessly. This was the first place I passed with alcohol," Lacey said, bringing my attention back to her. "I didn't feel like going home to sleep on a bed that I'd fucked him on the last time I'd been on it."

"How long were you together?" I asked, trying to get the image of her naked and moaning out of my head. I held her drink out, purposefully brushing my fingers over hers when she took it.

Her eyes darted to mine. "A—a year."

"And how much of that year were you unhappy?" I already knew, by the way her eyes dimmed and her hand gripped the glass, that it'd been a while. She'd been with the guy, but he clearly hadn't doted on her the way she deserved.

Not the way I could.

The fuck? Calm it down, Nate. You don't date or dote. You do quick fucks and lengthy fucks, dirty fucks, and sweet fucks. That's it. Period. End of story.

Lacey gave a hollow laugh that tugged at my stupid chest. "Nine months?"

Hell's tits, that was a long time to be miserable with someone. When was the last time she'd been kissed with actual heat, or laid out and consumed like an all-you-can-eat buffet?

"What's that look for?" she asked, raising her glass to

her lips.

Well, here went nothing. "I was just thinking about all that time you wasted with someone who didn't treat you right. That's a long time to not be seen, and a lot of nights to not be worshipped."

She choked, inhaling her sip and coughing. Her eyes watered, and she grabbed a napkin from the bar, dabbing at them. "Smooth. So, is this the part where you offer to show me what I've been missing out on?"

"If it was, I feel like now you've set me up for failure."

Her lips tightened like she was holding back a laugh, and I subconsciously learned toward her, desperate to hear it.

"Let me guess, you could show me how a man *should* treat me? Take me on a magic carpet ride?"

"Maybe."

She sat back, running her eyes up my body, and I didn't miss the way she shifted in her seat. "I've yet to find a man who can do anything to me better than I can do myself."

My pants got a little tighter at the image she'd just planted in my head. Of her sprawled across a bed, hips propped up on a pillow, working her fingers in and out of herself.

Fuck, I needed to clear that out real quick, or every person who saw me was going to have a damn good idea of what I was thinking about.

"Come here, and I'll let you in on a little secret, Lacey."

She quirked a perfectly penciled brow and pushed her

empty glass toward me before obliging. A faint peachy perfume emanated from her chest as she leaned forward, and it teased my senses, sending goosebumps down my arms.

What would it be like to pull one of her nipples in my mouth while that fruity smell invaded my nose? Paradise, that's what.

Snagging her glass, I began refilling it. "The truth is men rarely do anything better than women."

"That's no secret, Bart."

My hand froze on its way to hand her the drink, and I blinked. Then blinked again. There's no way she thought I looked like a fucking *Bart*. Right?

My pulse skyrocketed and my cock strained even harder against my jeans when the corner of her lips curled. She pushed up onto the bar, leaning across it toward my side.

Don't look at her breasts, don't look at her breasts, don't look at—God, she had such perfect tits. I bet her nipples peaked so fucking well.

I snapped my eyes back to her face, where they never should have left, and she had the nerve to wink at me as she stole the glass from my hand and returned to her seat.

Her pink hair slid off her shoulders as she knocked her head back, downing most of the drink in one go. A little leaked out from the corner of her mouth and dripped down her chin, sending me from aroused to solid fucking stone in an instant.

I wanted to run my tongue across her chin and taste the mixture of the tequila with the salt of her skin. Lay her out over the bar and work my way down her body, dribbling liquor across her lush waist and thighs so I could delve my tongue into every divot and curve and lick her clean.

A cough pulled me out of my daydream, and I focused on Lacey's face, realizing I'd been caught staring at her, yet again. I smiled wide, blatantly readjusting myself.

Her eyes tracked the movement, noticing the bulge I couldn't hide if I wanted to, and the tip of her tongue darted out to wet her lips.

"So," she said, clearing her throat and wiping her hand across her chin, "you admit that you fail at being better than a woman at anything?"

I held up a finger to hold that thought, and worked my way down the bar, refilling drinks. It gave me the minute I needed for my heart to return to normal and my dick to calm the fuck down.

Pouring a water on my way back, I handed it to her, and her grateful smile warmed me more than it should.

"To answer your question, Lacey, I'm a talented man in many areas. *Many*. But that's thanks to all the beautiful female souls who've shown me what I know."

"How so?"

"Well, if we're talking about all facets of my life, then my occupational success is thanks to a female teacher I had growing up, and the general quality of me as a person is thanks to my treasure of a mother."

I ran my thumb over my bottom lip, watching her eyes track it. "And I know just how to make a woman soak my sheets thanks to previous, open partners who weren't afraid to spell it out for me."

She sat back and swallowed, and I didn't fail to notice the way she squeezed her thighs together. "Have you always thought poorly about men, or are you just negative, overall, Bart?"

My left eye twitched at that ugly ass name again. "Not at all. I like to bend over for a good cock just like anyone attracted to them. I'm just also honest about shortcomings."

I analyzed her face to see her reaction to my open sexual preferences, but her eyes only heated, and she raised her glass. "Here's to daddy issues and men with shortcomings and short *comings*."

"Cheers to that, Lacey."

LIAR T JAMES

CHAPTER 5

Lacey

THE WARM QUIVER making its way up my spine was my sign that I needed to stop at two drinks. I'd never been much of a drinker to begin with, anyway. Working around drunk men most nights tended to dissuade me, so I was a bit of a lightweight.

But one look at that crooked grin, and I was already pushing my empty glass toward him for another. Just one more hour with him was all I needed, and then I'd take a car service home and get my car tomorrow.

He took my glass but set it in his sink instead of refilling it. "Sorry, Lacey, but last call already passed. We're

actually getting ready to close."

What? I snatched my phone off the counter, tapping the screen to see the time. Holy shit, I'd been here, chatting the night away with him for hours. I should've known, given I'd already had to walk to the bathroom twice just to shimmy life back into my ass cheeks.

I felt my face flush and dropped my head onto my arms to hide my embarrassment. God, he was probably miserable, unable to escape my annoying rambling.

"Yeah, unfortunately you came to a family-friendly restaurant on a Sunday. Not many people publicly drink away their sorrows here on a work night."

I rolled my head to the side so I could see him from the cradle of my arms. "Maybe I'll just walk my tipsy ass to the nearest seedy bar then."

His green eyes flashed. "Your life isn't my business, but I hope you don't, Lacey. Not everyone is as nice as you."

"I strip and dance naked for a living, I'm well aware how most people are." I snapped my mouth shut, my eyes widening at my unintentional slip. Yet another reason why I shouldn't drink in public. I had zero filter.

I watched his face, terrified of what I'd see. Derek's had turned from the sweet, rounded face I knew, to one of pure venom when he'd found out.

Bart's eyes stayed locked on mine, a small frown marring his otherwise neutral expression. "I'm sorry that's been your experience. People suck."

Unable to come up with a reasonable reply to his lack of shock or disgust, I brushed it off with a shrug and sat up to gulp down the water he'd brought me.

Sexy, funny, *and* respectful? Jesus, did the man have a single flaw?

He tapped the bar with his knuckles, his brow creased in thought. "I need to run to the back really quick." He turned to go, but stopped, adding, "Don't go anywhere."

I nodded. I had no plans of leaving until he made me. The only thing that awaited me at home was a silent apartment filled with items and memories I didn't want to keep.

I hadn't lied when I'd told him I hadn't been happy in my relationship for a while. Having to hide what I did because of how judgmental Derek was had been exhausting.

He'd had no problem urging me to keep an apartment I couldn't afford on the part of town *he* liked, yet he hadn't possessed the tiniest thread of sympathy for how hard it was for me to pay for it.

I'd pathetically stayed with him anyway, ignoring the red flags, because the alternative had been too depressing. I was a social butterfly; I didn't like being alone.

"What's on your mind?"

I jumped, almost falling off the stool when Bart's voice came from directly behind me. I whipped around to come face to face with his chest.

Damn, his tattoos were even hotter up close. I had to grip the edge of my seat to keep from reaching out and tracing the outline of a shattered skull inked on his left forearm.

"I was thinking about how I don't want to go home.

It's going to be quiet, and I'll just be alone in my thoughts."

He stepped between my stool and the one next to me, leaning his side against the bar. "Then don't."

"As you've pointed out, there's not a whole lot of non-seedy places to spend the night at on a Sunday, Bart."

His smile shriveled as his lip curled. "Must you call me that?"

"Well, you're not wearing a name tag, Bartender. And honestly, at this point, I'm pretty attached to Bart, so I think I'll stick with it."

Clarity crossed his face, and he shook his head, chuckling. "Well, *Lacey*, after quite an irritating start to my day, I'm ready to get the hell out of here. I cut a deal with a friend to cover my closing duties, so I'm headed home."

"Oh." I knew I wasn't exactly this guy's type, not any guy's type according to Derek, but damn. For a minute there, I'd thought maybe I'd been wrong.

I forced a smile to my face. "All right, no worries. I hope you have a nice night," I said, moving to hide my embarrassment by sliding off the stool and smoothing out my skirt.

A warm touch to my arm had me freezing mid-shift, and my eyes flicked down to the fingers cupped around my elbow before raising to his face.

His lips tipped up on one side, and he leaned toward me, causing a few black strands of hair to hang over his forehead.

"I live in the neighborhood across the street. Would you like to join me, Miss Lace?"

The quickness with which I wanted to shout, "Yes," should've been my indicator I was in way over my head. But I held back my response, unsure what his motive for asking might be.

Did he truly not care that I spread my legs in front of people's faces for a living? Or did he assume, like Derek had, that it also meant I was a prostitute? Because if he offered to pay me, I'd kick his balls all the way up to his lungs.

"Are you only asking me because I told you I'm a stripper?"

He pulled back, frowning down at me, "Why would that have anything to do with it?"

I shrugged, suddenly uncomfortable. "In my experience, people tend to have certain…assumptions when they find out."

"Guessing your ex fell into that category?"

"Yeah."

Bart sucked on his teeth, turning to stare out the window for a moment. "I don't expect a damn thing from you."

Okay, that one stung a little. Grabbing my purse, I gave him a half-hearted thumbs up. "Understood."

He stepped closer, but he didn't touch me. He just stood there, close enough that I could feel his breath coast across my face. "You misunderstand me, Lacey-Lu."

His eyes dipped to my lips, and I instinctively darted my tongue out to wet them. Was it warm in here?

"There is nothing I want more than to end this night nestled between those gorgeous fucking thighs of yours, but I don't *expect* it from you."

I gripped my purse tighter, my breathing so erratic that my voice came out raspy. "And if I want that too?"

He smiled, and I swore the man could impregnate me with that look alone.

"Then I'll happily spend the rest of the night seeing how many times I can get you to orgasm before your body gives out."

CHAPTER 6

Bartender

THIS WAS NOT my first rodeo, nor was it my second. Hell, I'd been in rodeos with a pen full of players. Sometimes I was the rider and sometimes I was the bull. I'd literally done everything under the sun.

So why did my skin feel like it was about to vibrate clean off my body at just the sight of Lacey walking next to me? I felt as nervous and excited as I had as a teenager about to get my dick wet for the first time.

Forcing myself to take her all the way home before touching her was taking every bit of strength I had. I could only hope she was feeling at least a sliver of the same

attraction and craze as I was.

My eyes gravitated to her for the tenth time in three minutes. She'd looked so horrified when she'd told me what she did for a living, as if she fully expected me to throw her to the curb rather than take her home.

As if a confident woman comfortable with her body wasn't the sexiest fucking thing to walk the planet.

My mind unwillingly jumped to the ex she'd mentioned. The ex who I had a feeling had taken that delicious confidence and twisted it.

If I was right, I was going to have to play tonight a little differently, and I'd be lying if I said I wasn't excited as hell about it.

Clearing my throat, I nudged her with my shoulder. "If you don't mind me asking, what happened between you and your ex? I know you said you fought about your job, but if you'd been together for so long before that…"

Bringing him up might very well backfire, and it was truly none of my business, but I couldn't seem to refrain from digging into her life. I wanted to find a hole, or even the smallest crevice, and bury myself into it.

I refused to analyze what that feeling meant.

"We had, yeah. He really wasn't awful, and we got along well," she said. "But then he showed his true colors, and it turned out, I didn't like the same shades he did."

I nudged her again, just for the excuse to touch her. "I have zero experience with relationships, so I guess I'm just struggling to understand your situation. Why'd you stay with someone you had to lie to?"

She gave me a penetrating look like she was trying to see into my fucking soul. "You don't date?"

"No."

"At all?"

"I love. I touch. I devour. I repeat," I said, forcing myself to meet her gaze, and telling myself it was to make sure she understood what tonight was, not because I feared her reaction.

But she only nodded, facing forward again. "I stayed with him because he was comfortable, I guess. I didn't lie about *where* I worked. He knew I was a waitress there. I didn't start dancing until after we'd been together a few months."

She kicked a rock out of her path, frowning at the ground. "I knew how he'd feel about it, but I was desperate. I could barely afford to eat, let alone live on his side of town and accompany him to all the events he attended.

"Even dancing, I still struggle most months, just nothing like I had. And the longer I went without telling him, the easier it was to convince myself not to."

I cupped my hand around her elbow, slowing her pace, and directed her onto the driveway we'd reached. "How did he find out?"

She laughed, but it was a dead, humorless sound. "He showed up this evening for a bachelor party. I didn't even know he'd been invited to one and wasn't prepared at all. He saw me on stage, and it got ugly."

"Did he hurt you?" I asked, immediately thinking of Madison. I didn't know anything concrete, but my gut had always said she'd been hurt. Bad. And the thought of Lacey also going through something like that made my blood boil.

"No, nothing like that. Don't get me wrong, Derek turned out to be a stuck up, judgmental asshole, but he never laid a hand on me."

"So, what happened?"

"He yelled at me in front of the entire establishment about how much of a whore and a slut I was. The bouncers had to throw him out, and I ended up taking the rest of tonight off."

I froze a few feet from my front steps, tipping my head back and staring up at the night sky. "Fucking idiot."

"Excuse me?" she said, shock bleeding into her tone. Her assumption that I was calling *her* the idiot said everything it needed to about how that garbage truck of a man had made her view herself.

I looked back down at her, admiring the way my porch light hit her, lighting up her face like a beacon in the night.

"He's an idiot, Lacey. If his goal was to insult you, he failed. Calling you a slut isn't an insult. A woman with a high sexual appetite and a healthy relationship with her body are qualities a partner should desire."

She blinked at me like a deer in headlights, and it broke my heart a little. My Lacey-Lu had no idea the power she could gain with the right partner.

She stepped past me to stand in front of my door,

tilting her head when she noticed the garden gnome I had perched next to it.

"It's admirable."

"My gnome?" I asked, well aware that my handmade décor was not what she was referring to. I reached around her to unlock the door, brushing the front of my body across her backside.

She tensed. "The bubble you live in. The real world doesn't think the way you do. *Especially* about people like me."

Instead of opening the door, I gripped her hips and spun her, pushing her back against the wood. She gasped, and her eyes went wide as saucers.

I let my gaze caress down her body, trailing my fingertips up her arms and across her shoulders. Her skin pebbled beneath my touch, and I bit back a groan. She was already so receptive.

Leaning down to hover my face above her neck, I inhaled deeply, drinking in her fruity perfume. God, I wanted to run my tongue over her skin and steal a taste.

"I could help you, you know."

Her chest rose and fell rapidly at my words, and her voice came out soft and breathy. "Help me do what, exactly?"

"Take back the power he stole from you."

CHAPTER 7

Lacey

I WATCHED HIM bend his knee, lifting his foot to kick back against the door and shut it behind him. The sound seemed to echo out in an otherwise silent home, heightening my nerves.

He tossed his keys onto a table just inside his home, simultaneously shoving the toes of one foot into the heel of the other to work his shoe off. I tracked his movements as he did the other, feeling like a panther viewing its prey before pouncing.

Why was a man walking around the house barefoot so attractive?

I tore my eyes from him as he removed his jacket and looked around his home to prevent myself from jumping his bones right then and there. What I saw took my breath away.

When he'd said he lived across the street, I figured he'd meant in an apartment of some kind. He was an unmarried bartender at a chicken wing restaurant, making what I assumed to be around minimum wage. An apartment made sense.

But what I entered was a pristine, two-story home that didn't match him at all. It looked like a professional had designed it for a television series with white walls, gray-washed wood floors, and dark trim work.

His furniture matched the same theme. If it weren't for the bright pops of color in his wall paintings and throw pillows, the house would've looked like it was pulled straight out of a black and white film. I was in love with it.

I was draping my own jacket across his entry table, when a noise behind me caught my attention. I glanced over my shoulder to see Bart at a standalone bar, holding two shot glasses and a bottle of tequila.

He looked so out of place in his home that I couldn't help but smile at the view. I'd been expecting a bachelor pad with condoms and beer bottles everywhere, but what I found proved Mr. Bartender was more than he seemed.

"Like what you see?" he asked.

I was about to poke at his pride with a verbal dagger just to see what he'd do, but he wiggled his eyebrows at me in the most ridiculous way, and a laugh burst out of me.

It felt foreign and rough, like shaking out an old coat that'd been stuffed in the attic for months. There was nothing quiet or dainty about it, and it felt *good*.

His face went slack, and his body shifted toward me just enough that he missed the shot glass and splashed liquor on himself. He blinked rapidly, setting the bottle down to grab a napkin off the bar.

I shook my head, continuing to laugh softly as he wiped at his wrist. I walked up to him and reached an arm out, brushing it against his as I lifted the bottle and poured the second shot.

Looking him straight in the eyes, I picked it up and knocked it back, letting the burn bolster my confidence. "How do you plan on touching me tonight, Bart? Will you roll into me soft and sweet like we're making love? Or are you a sweaty, skin clapping, hip bones smacking kinda guy?"

His eyes heated, and he dropped the soiled napkin to follow my lead and down the other shot. "Sex isn't an either/or situation, Lacey. It's a spectrum that I plan to slide your pussy up and down depending on what you need."

Jesus fucking Christ. If he kept that up, I'd be at orgasm number one before we even did anything. "And what exactly do you think I require, Bartender?"

"I think you need to be treated like the dirty slut you are."

"Excuse me?" Out of every sentence he could have

uttered, that wasn't at all what I'd expected him to say.

"I think you need someone to call you every single thing he did while you scream and ride out your pleasure. They're only nasty words when used by fragile men. They can also give you power. You just have to own them."

I stood there with my mouth hanging open like a fish on a line. I'd never thought about it that way before, but...the idea already had my inner muscles clenching. Anything to get this man to touch me.

Taking advantage of my stunned silence, he raised an arm over his shoulder, fisting his shirt and pulling it up over his head to expose his entire upper half.

Holy tattoos. They weren't just on his arms. His entire chest was covered in them as well, and I nearly salivated at the way his muscles shifted underneath them. Resisting the urge to climb him like a tree and lick each one was one of the hardest things I've ever done.

"Or," he continued, tossing his shirt to the ground, "I could be wrong. And in that case, I can make love to you soft and sweet. If that's what you'd prefer."

"I don't." The words flew out of my mouth before he'd even finished speaking, and I flushed, embarrassed by my eagerness. But damn, I didn't want sweet.

I wanted exactly what he was offering. I wanted him fast and hard and filthy. And if that meant crawling across the floor while he called me Fido, then I was more than game.

Logically, I knew it didn't make sense for me to trust

anything he said, but I did. For whatever reason, I believed that no matter what happened tonight, he'd respect me both during and after.

He hummed to himself, gently prying the empty glass from my hand and setting it next to his. He walked forward, the heat of his body teasing me when he stopped mere inches from me.

"Then why don't you put us both out of our misery and tell me exactly what you want."

I rubbed my hands down my sides, hoping the movement hid the way they were shaking. "I don't want sweet. Not even close."

His answer was to thread one hand through my hair, gripping the back of my neck, while the other wrapped around my lower back. Pulling my body firmly into his, his eyes dropped to my lips, and he lowered his head.

It wasn't so much a kiss as it was sharing breath. He hovered, his lips no more than a featherlight touch on my own. "Well then, Miss Lace, I shall make love to you dirty."

And then he smashed his lips to mine.

CHAPTER 8

Lacey

WITH MY BODY flush with his, I was slapped with two polar opposites—the careful, gentle hold of his hands and the hard length pressed into my stomach. I didn't stand a chance.

He angled my head, positioning me where he wanted and taking no prisoners. He attacked me, eating from my mouth and running his tongue over mine in firm, demanding strokes.

My eyes rolled back at the taste of him, and my body arched, seeking more. I had a feeling that tongue was going to be the death of me by the end of the night.

As if he knew exactly what I was thinking, he chuckled against my lips, shifting his body so he could grind his thigh between mine.

"God, Bart—"

His teeth latched onto my bottom lip, pulling it into his mouth and silencing me. He bit down, and the pressure of it trailed all the way to my toes. My hips moved of their own accord, matching his movements until I was moaning into his mouth, humping him right smack in the middle of his home.

I'd just found a rhythm, his thigh pressing into my clit at the perfect angle, when the hand at my waist suddenly disappeared. He drew back, pulling an embarrassingly desperate whine from my throat.

I didn't even need to feel his raging hard-on to know he was just as affected by me as I was by him. His chest moved up and down rapidly, and his eyes were hooded and dark as he ran them over my face.

"Ruby."

I blinked. "What?"

"That's what I want you to say if our game stops being fun. If I go too far, or if you just don't like it anymore, you say 'ruby'. Anything else will be part of the game. Do you understand?"

I nodded, my throat feeling dry.

"No," he said, tapping a finger under my chin in reprimand. "I need to hear it, Lacey. If you tell me I'm being too rough, I will only fuck you harder. I will not stop for *any other word.* Do you understand?"

Nervous was an understatement. I was nervous, excited, slightly irritated, aroused, everything. It was overwhelming. I needed the fucking release this man was promising me.

"Ruby. I understand."

"Good girl." He caressed his palm over my cheek and smiled down at me before moving it to the back of my head again.

He grabbed a fistful of my hair and yanked so that my neck arched up for him. Leaning down, his breath coasted over my lips. "Now get on your knees and beg for my cock."

I bit my tongue, waiting for a punchline that never came. Was he serious?

Anger soared inside me, heating my neck all the way to my ears, and I had to close my eyes and breathe. I didn't know this man, hell, we hadn't even swapped names, and he wanted me to *beg?* I'd never begged a man for anything in my life, and that included Derek.

Yet here my one-night stand stood, expecting me to do it for his cock? Just like that?

"Yes, Lacey. Just…like…that," he said, making me realize I'd spoken that last part out loud. I opened my eyes to give him a piece of my mind, but just as quickly as my anger had risen, it dissipated the moment I met his heated gaze.

He wasn't looking at me with a single hint of arrogance or condemnation. Pupils blown out, brows lowered, and lips parted, he looked at me like an addict awaiting their fix. Like I was both his damnation and salvation all at once.

As if, even though *he* was ordering *me* to my knees, he was more than willing to crawl on his own for me if I asked.

I fucking loved it. I craved his claim almost as much as I craved his touch. I wanted to feel powerful over the words Derek had thrown at me. To feel strong and confident, both in and out of the bedroom.

I wanted to be this man's whore, and not a single bit of me felt ashamed.

He smiled, seeming to be aware of the epiphany going on in my head the same way he'd somehow understood everything else about me tonight.

The hand gripping my hair pulled harder. "Tell me what you want."

"I want your cock."

He released me, clucking his tongue. "I'm not sure you do. Consider me unconvinced."

My nostrils flared, but I swallowed back my retort and lowered myself to my knees, the toes of my heels scraping across the floor as I did.

Leaning forward, I ran my tongue up the crotch of his jeans until it met the trail of hair that disappeared beneath his waistband. "I want your cock in my mouth, Bartender," I said, pressing my palm along the bulge hidden behind the dark denim. "I need it."

I worked the button out and then dropped my fingers to grasp his zipper. I looked up at him as I pulled it down, the sound of the separating threads heightening the tension already pulsing around us.

He exhaled heavily. "Yeah?"

I bit my lip and nodded, curling my fingers over the band of his jeans. I eased them down his legs, trying not to panic at what I saw as I helped him step out of them. Then I moved to his boxers, scraping my nails along his skin as I repeated the process and freed him of those as well.

Mother of God, he was going to split me in two. My eyes widened at the size of him, my inner muscles clenching around nothing, somehow both scared and eager to have him inside me.

I wrapped a hand around the base of his thick shaft, watching a bead of liquid appear at his tip as I gave him a few teasing pumps. His entire body stiffened in response, and he fisted his hands at his sides like it was taking all his self-control not to touch me.

"That's it. Come on, Lacey, I want to see you swallow me like the good little whore you are." His voice had somehow grown even huskier, and my pussy practically throbbed in answer.

Fluttering my eyelashes, I moved closer and licked the droplet from his tip. The salty musk of him exploded across my tongue, and I gave a sharp suck, swirling my tongue around him, and enjoying the way he hissed through his teeth. The sound inflamed my bravado, encouraging me to take more.

I rolled my lips over my teeth, moving slow at first, and

trying not to dislocate my jaw as my throat acclimated to the massive invasion. The urge to gag was overpowering, but I took my time, relaxing as much as possible while pumping my hand over the part I hadn't yet taken.

He groaned when I ran my tongue along the underside, his raspy voice making it almost a growl, and it spurred me on. I uncovered my teeth to gently graze them down his length, and the control he'd been hanging on to, snapped.

His hands dove into my hair, and he gripped both sides of my head, holding me in place, as he began fucking my throat. Carefully at first, then he picked up speed, filling the room with the sloppy sound of his cock rutting into my mouth.

He grunted with a deep thrust, hitting the back of my throat and making me choke around him. "Goddamn, Lacey."

He pulled back just enough that I could breathe again and stared at me in awe, running his hand over my hair like I was something to be revered. "Look at you. You're taking me so well. I could fuck your mouth all night."

I made a panicked noise around his shaft. He wasn't serious, right? My jaw was already screaming at me. He smirked, easing himself in and out in shallow thrusts.

"Don't worry, Lacey-Lu. I fully intend on turning your pussy into a masterpiece tonight. But first, I want to coat that whip of a tongue and watch it slide down your pretty throat."

He steadied my head, and it was my only warning

before he slammed forward. I gagged hard, digging my nails into his hips as tears spilled over and ran down my face.

"Shh, it's okay. Inhale through your nose and swallow—yeah, baby, just like that."

I looked up at the endearment to see his head tipped back and his eyes squeezed closed. His grip in my hair tightened, and a shudder worked through him.

It set me on fucking fire. Maybe I truly was a whore because his pleasure only further fueled my own. I didn't just want to please him, I wanted to see him come completely *undone*.

I dug my nails in harder, pulling his attention back down to me. Then I sat back on my heels, resting my hands in my lap, and opened my mouth as far as it would go.

His eyes flared, seeming more black than green, and his fingers twitched like it was taking everything in him not to shove me down and fuck me into the floor.

"Fucking hell, Lacey. The sight of you like this just might make me believe in God."

He widened his stance, cradling my head, and gave me a single warning squeeze before burying himself straight to the back of my throat.

CHAPTER 9

Bartender

I'D TOLD MYSELF I wouldn't touch her, not until *she* touched me first. I was going to let her make the first move to be sure she was truly interested in what I was offering.

But then she'd looked up at me from under those long lashes, uttering the exact words I wanted to hear while her peach scent tickled my nose, and I was gone.

Another jolt of pleasure shot down my spine as I moved in and out of her perfect mouth. Failure never felt so fucking good.

I pumped harder, punishing her for not having come into my life sooner. Her nails drew blood at my hips and

tears ran down her face, but that glorious creature took it.

And the best part about how well she was doing, was how much I was going to enjoy rewarding her afterward. If she thought her throat was sore now, it was going to be raw by the time she finished screaming tonight.

I couldn't hold back the moan that slipped past my lips at the thought, and I released her hair, forcing myself to slow down. I needed to maintain control, because if I didn't, she'd end up beneath me, and this night would be over much faster than I planned.

Her blue eyes widened, and she placed both hands against my torso, pulling away. Gooseflesh spread across my skin from the abrupt change in temperature against my cock. The chill of the air biting after the heat of her mouth.

"Did I tell you to stop?" I asked, feeling my balls tighten at the sight of her. Her lips were still parted, her cheeks flushed, and mascara streamed down her face from the onslaught I'd just forced upon her.

Her brow creased, uncertainty fogging her expression. "You seemed like you were trying not to—"

"I know my limits, Lacey. And my limit is that I'm not fucking done until your face is a goddamn mess."

Her cheeks deepened to a beautiful red hue, whether from excitement or anger, I didn't know. Likely the latter.

My pulse thrummed in my veins, wondering how much she'd willingly take from me before she said the word and tapped out of the fun. But Lacey stayed silent and submissive, nearly making me bust my load right there.

Leaning down, I ran my fingers over her lips, smearing her lipstick further. "Now spit on it and keep going."

She glared. "Unless your end goal is tickling my fucking stomach, I can't take you any deeper."

I *tsk*ed, giving her a warning pat to her cheek. "You're here to take me like the slut you are, not run your mouth."

Her eyes flashed, and her lips peeled back to spew something I'd certainly have to spank her for. And as much as I *really* wanted to do that, I wasn't ready to see her off her knees just yet.

So, before she could speak, I grabbed her chin with one hand and yanked on her hair with my other, gaping her mouth for me.

"I said, I want you *messy*." And then, in a complete asshole move that had me mentally apologizing to my mother, I spit on her tongue.

She bucked, trying to pull away from me, but I just hauled her up and smashed my lips to hers, sucking her tongue into my mouth.

She tasted like a mixture of tequila and me, and I knew right then I wanted more. I needed to taste every part of her like I needed air to breathe.

Refusing to let go, I dominated her mouth, nipping and sucking at her lips like a man possessed. And only when her fight died out and she relaxed in my hold, gasping for breath, did I pull away.

I released her chin, trailing my fingertips across her cheek and pushing her hair out of her eyes. She was so fucking beautiful, it hurt.

I'd barely gripped my shaft again, about to order her to get ready, when she glared at me, spit right on my dick, and opened wide.

Fuck. "That's my girl."

I didn't make it more than two minutes after that. She followed my instructions just as well as I knew she would, and the wet sound of my cock moving over her tongue was my breaking point.

My orgasm hit me like a freight train, shooting down my spine as I rammed into her mouth one final time. Her eyes flew open, and her throat convulsed around me as she swallowed again and again.

I'd done and seen a lot of things over the years, but seeing the mixture of cum and spit string from her mouth as I pulled free might've made the top spot on my list of favorites.

"You're perfect."

She licked her lips, wincing slightly, and winked at me. Fucking winked.

I immediately reached down and gripped her arms, pulling her to her feet. She wobbled as she stood, legs shaky from how long she'd knelt on the hard floor. I grinned, wrapping my arms around her, and captured her swollen lips.

She responded enthusiastically, threading her hands into my hair, and fisting it at the roots. My eyes burned as she yanked, but I just kissed her harder, living for the taste of her mouth. It was even better when it was laced with me.

I began walking her backward into the living room, our kiss turning into more of a clash of teeth as we moved. It wasn't smooth or graceful, but I maintained contact, unwilling to part from her until we stood a foot away from my couch.

Giving her one final press of my lips, I gripped her hips and spun her, facing her back to me. "You made a mess of me, Lacey," I said, nipping her earlobe. "Now I'm going to eat yours."

"Who says I'm a mess? Maybe choking on a dick doesn't do it for me," she gasped, even as she pushed back and rubbed her ass against me.

I removed my hands from her hips, pulling one back to smack the side of her ass. She jumped, squeaking out a curse.

"Don't lie to me," I said, running my tongue up the column of her neck, "or I'll have to punish you."

She tipped her head farther, giving me more access. "Promise?"

I kissed her shoulder in answer. "You know, I'd planned on making you strip for me. I wanted to see every move you let everyone else see," I said, easing the zipper of her skirt down. "But I'm no longer feeling patient enough for that."

I worked her skirt down her thighs, letting it fall to her feet, and was rewarded with an eyeful of bare skin. I had to forcibly clench my jaw to keep myself from taking a bite.

She wore no panties, just a bodysuit that covered only a few inches of two perfect cheeks. I ran my hands over them, groping and squeezing as I did. I appreciated the entire human body, but I was one hundred percent an ass man. And this one? I wanted to fucking eat it.

"Fucking hell, Lacey."

I moved one hand between her legs to undo where the crotch of her top buttoned between them. The fabric was drenched and her thighs slick against my hand from her arousal.

I licked my lips in anticipation, murmuring against her neck. "Naughty girl, if I'd have known you liked sucking my cock so much, I wouldn't have stopped."

She only made a breathy huff in response, rotating her hips and trying to gain any bit of friction from my fingers.

I made quick work of her top, helping her out of it and tossing it to the floor as I admired her smooth, unblemished back. It was like the perfect canvas, filling me with more ideas than I could possibly make happen in a single night.

"No bra?" I asked, gliding my hands around to her soft belly and making my way up to cup her full, heavy breasts.

She shook her head, making her hair tickle my face. "The ones I wear for work are miserable, so I tend to avoid wearing any outside of it."

"Lucky me." I kissed along her neck and across her shoulder, rolling her nipples between my fingers. She moaned, arching her back and pushing them into my hands, silently begging for more.

"Here's what's going to happen," I said, pinching her peaked tips and bringing a deeper, more urgent, sound out of her. "I'm going to lie back on this couch, and you're going to ride me like the whore you are."

Her body stiffened, and she twisted her head to look back at me, brows furrowed. "You want me to—"

I wrapped a hand around her jaw, forcing her to see the naked desire in my eyes. "Yes, Lacey," I said, moving my other hand between her thighs, "because you took me so goddamn well, and now I'm fucking starving for this pussy."

CHAPTER 10

Lacey

SEEING HIM SPRAWLED across his couch in nothing but his birthday suit had all kinds of thoughts running through my mind. The first and foremost being that I wanted to straddle his hips and stuff myself like a Thanksgiving turkey.

"Are you just going to stand there and tease me with dessert, or are you going to feed me, Miss Lace?"

I subconsciously pressed my legs together at the gravelly tone of his voice, and my heart picked up its pace. "I've never done…I mean, I've done *this*, but not this way. I'm not exactly light."

"Your body is perfect."

I looked down and fidgeted. I wasn't necessarily self-conscious—I literally showed my body for a living—but that didn't mean I wasn't aware I was curvier than society's impossible standard for beauty.

The people I danced for didn't go to the club looking for perfection, and I certainly didn't sit on their faces. They were there to get drunk and see titties. This was different in about every possible way.

"Look at me."

I flicked my eyes up at his command to see him gripping his cock, already thick and hard again.

"See what you do to me?" he said, moving his hand up and down. "Now get your ass over here and take a seat."

Was I nervous? Yes. But I wasn't insane. I sure as hell wasn't going to make the man tell me a third time.

Placing a knee on the edge of the couch, I raised my other leg up and over, straddling his waist. His fist bumped against my back as he continued to pump himself, and his eyes seared into me, telling me to *move it*.

Yes, sir. I crawled up, placing my hands on the armrest above him, and raised my body. I'd barely positioned myself over his head when he lost patience and lifted his face to meet me.

The first flick of his tongue had me uttering sounds I didn't even know I could make, and the second licked all the shame right out of me. By the third hard-tipped flick, I stopped giving a shit about being quiet.

He took his time, humming with satisfaction when I cursed or moaned. He seemed to be enjoying it as much as I was and continued to swipe his tongue through me again and again like I was his favorite fucking ice cream.

My entire body shuddered at the sensations he was creating, and I dug my fingers into the couch trying to fight the urge to roll my hips and maintain my position above him.

Holy hell. I tensed, and my arms shook as I tried to relax enough for my orgasm to crest while also supporting my weight. The last thing I needed was to suffocate the guy.

Mid-stroke, he suddenly stopped. Wrapping both his hands around my thighs, he dug his fingers in and shoved me up. I glanced down in shock, terrified I'd already ruined the night, and was pinned in place by a set of angry green eyes.

"Don't you dare hold back, Lacey. I said to take a seat and fucking *ride* me. Hover again, and I'll spank your ass 'til it's raw." He tightened his hold and yanked me back down, taking my clit between his teeth and sucking it into his mouth.

I cried out, gouging my nails into the armrest, and rolled my hips back to give him better access. He groaned when his nose buried into me, and the vibration echoed through my clit, heightening the tingle he'd already built with each brutal swipe of his tongue.

He worked me like it was his sole purpose in life, noting my tells and adjusting his speed and pressure until I was a writhing mess, bucking and screaming for mercy.

"Oh fuck, oh fuck."

"That's it, Lacey, give it to me." He curled an arm around my hip, reaching down to rub firmly against my clit, right as he thrust his tongue inside me.

I broke, pressing down and grinding on his face with no reserve, and he didn't waste a second. He fucking devoured me, licking and sucking like he'd die without it. And even after he'd lapped up every bit of my release, he didn't stop.

"Holy shit." My entire body was shaking as I came down, and I held the couch for dear life, trying not to roll clean off in my post-orgasm high. I honestly wasn't sure if I could even feel my legs at that point.

Grabbing my hips, he suddenly shifted me forward, knocking me off balance. I felt him slide out from under me and move back, leaving me kneeling with my elbows on the armrest.

I looked over my shoulder to ask what he was doing, but before I could so much as open my mouth, he shoved on the center of my back, forcing my face down.

Cheek pressed into the fabric, I couldn't see him, but the cushion rose and fell as he settled somewhere behind me. There was a brief, tense pause, and then his fingers were sliding through my pussy. He took his time, spreading me open, and I felt the pressure of two more start to push into me. Slowly. So fucking slowly.

"You like being my whore, don't you, Lacey?"

I nodded. If being a whore meant getting orgasms like *that?* Fuck yes. I'd be his whore and own that shit.

He leaned up, smacking me on the ass and making me yelp from the unexpected sting. "Say it. Tell me what you are."

"I'm a whore."

He pulled his fingers out to their tips just to slam them back in, rocking my body forward. "Wrong," he said, pulling them out again only to work in a third. He almost seemed to growl as he stuffed me full, angrily pumping them in and out of me in a punishing rhythm.

Why was he angry? I'd said exactly what he'd told me to. "What—" I began, but my words cut off when the hand spreading me moved up between my ass cheeks. He pushed one out as far as he could, and then I felt the wet heat of his tongue slide up between them.

I stiffened, lurching forward in surprise, but he pinned me in place, refusing to let me budge even an inch.

The fingers inside me never stopped their assault, brushing over my G-spot again and again until I felt another life-altering quake start to build.

"Tell me what you are, Lacey," he repeated, spitting on the exposed rim of my ass and using his tongue to glide it around the entrance like lube.

My eyes widened, and I instinctively clenched despite how good it felt. I wasn't innocent by any means, but Jesus Christ, he was *there*.

"I will edge you for hours, denying you as many

orgasms as I have to until you tell me what I want to hear," he warned, flicking his tongue harder.

He eased his fingers out of my pussy and circled them over my swollen clit, wetting it with my own arousal and sending stars into my vision.

"I *did*," I cried, my entire body vibrating with the need to break again. I was so close. "I said it! I'm a whore, I'm your whore, just—please!"

"Damn right you are," he said, removing his face from where he'd buried it to rim me. "Mine."

Then he pushed his pinkie into my ass right as his other hand pinched my clit, and I erupted.

My orgasm hit me harder than any I'd ever felt in my life—from myself or anyone else—and I screamed. His name, God's name, hell, I might have even called him daddy. All I knew was that my mind was a mess of pieces that I had no desire to ever put back together.

"Delicious," he murmured, pressing his face back in to lap at me one last time.

I slumped over the arm of the couch, my legs no longer capable of holding me up. It caused my ass to stick straight up in the air, but I didn't give a shit. His face was just back there anyway, let him look.

"Do you work tomorrow?"

The question caught me off guard, bringing my destroyed mind back to the present. He wanted to talk about my job? After *that*? And here I was hoping he was about to suggest marriage.

Still unable to comprehend how to use words yet, I simply bobbed my head, mumbling incoherently.

"Good," he said, pulling me back and helping me to my feet. He smirked at my teetering, disheveled self and kissed me on the forehead. The act was so unexpected and gentle, you'd have thought we'd be spending the night cuddling rather than fucking.

"Follow me." Without waiting to see if I'd listen, he turned, walking toward his staircase and heading up without a care in the world, buck ass naked.

I watched him ascend, knowing right then and there, I was in way over my head. Tonight was only a one-night stand for him. He'd made that abundantly clear. It'd started out that way for me, too, but now I wasn't so sure.

Because he was making me feel things I'd never felt before—powerful, sexy, worthy—and I liked it. I liked *him*. And I had a feeling the longer I stayed with him, the more at risk I would be of wanting to keep him.

CHAPTER 11

Lacey

DEREK AND I had been together for a year, but not once had I ever felt comfortable enough with him to wander my apartment naked when he was over. Maybe to walk out of the shower to my closet or to grab a water after sex, yes. But never like this.

I unclasped the straps of my heels, stepping out of them and groaning as I flexed my toes. It was almost as satisfying as taking my bra off after a long shift. I wasn't sure if Bart wanted me to keep them on, but I had no desire to follow him up the stairs in stilettos, only to trip and tumble back down, naked.

When I reached the second floor, he was waiting for me at the end of a short hallway to my right. He was leaned back against a closed door with his arms crossed over his chest, and he smiled when I came into view, trailing his eyes up my body.

His undisguised desire seared into me, lighting me on fire. I'd never felt more beautiful than I did when this man looked at me like that. Like he couldn't believe *he* was lucky enough to have a night with *me*.

"I want to show you something," he said, pushing off the door and turning to unlock it.

I raised my brows, walking down the hall to stand just behind him. "If this room is full of toys and whips, let me tell you now, I don't need an NDA, I'm all in."

He laughed, leaving the key in the lock and twisting the doorknob. "Lacey, if I had you all to myself in a room like that for a night, I'd have you screaming out 'ruby' so much, you'd think it was your name."

"Then I formally request two nights."

His nostrils flared, and the knob protested under his grip. "Careful what you ask for, Miss Lace." He pushed the door open, stepping in to flip on the light, and gestured for me to enter.

An intelligent woman would've refused to walk into a strange man's room that locked from the outside. However, given that this particular stranger had already licked all the common sense clean out of me, my ass walked right in.

I wasn't sure what I expected a restaurant bartender to

keep behind a locked door on the second floor of his model home, but what I saw definitely wouldn't have made the list.

The room was huge, more than double the size of my small bedroom at home, with white tile floor and matching white walls. There was a large, floor-to-ceiling window taking up most of the back wall, but other than that, every other wall was adorned in a plethora of art.

Paintings, drawings, black and white photos, shelves with sculptures, you name it. The man had an entire art gallery in his home. I slowly spun in place, mouth hanging open, ogling every unique piece.

Each was beautiful in its own way, but it was a piece displayed near the back that caught my eye. From the doorway it looked like an old-fashioned print of clasped weathered hands, but as I walked closer, I realized it wasn't a photo at all, but a painting.

"Wow," I whispered, running my fingers over the frame.

"Do you like it?"

"I've never seen a painting so realistic before. The detail is phenomenal." I squinted down at the corner, trying to make out the signature. "Is it authentic?"

"I certainly hope so." He chuckled, pulling my gaze away from the scribbled name.

Standing against a white wall, the colors of his tattoos appeared to pop, much like the art around him. It made him seem unreal, like he was just another perfect piece displayed in a room full of beauty.

"Why? Was it expensive?" I asked. He smiled wider at my question, drawing an answering grin to my own face. "Why are you laughing at me?"

"It's mine."

"I figured that much out myself there, Bart."

"No, I mean, it's *mine*. I'd planned to auction it off, but that one in particular took me months to finish. By the time it was done, I just couldn't bring myself to sell it." He shrugged, as if what he'd said was as casual as stating it was a breezy day.

"You made this?"

He nodded.

"Like…as in all of these?"

He pushed off the wall, sauntering over with a secret smile that was only for me. I gobbled it up like a starving woman, letting him pull my naked body in his arms.

"Why do you sound so surprised?" he asked, brushing his nose along my jaw. "Did you really think all I did was pour drinks at a wing joint?"

"Kind of."

His lips replaced his nose, leaving delicate, sweet kisses all the way up to my ear. "I feel like I should take offense."

"No," I somehow got out, "it's just unreal to meet someone who's this talented."

"I thought I'd already proven that earlier," he said, nipping at my earlobe.

I laughed, shoving against his bare chest. "Artistically

inclined. Is that better?"

He only smiled, gripping my hips and twisting me so that his dick pressed up against my ass and his arms circled my waist.

I swallowed, trying to maintain my train of thought, when all I could think about was the way he was squeezing me against him. "I guess I don't understand why you bother working there at all when you can do *this*."

He hummed against my shoulder. "Art is fulfilling and pays the bills, but it's also quite lonely, Lacey. I like people. Bartending satisfies that need."

"I guess all this explains your house."

"What about it?" he asked, picking my hair up off my shoulders and finger combing it together. My heart fluttered at the gentle touch. It felt so normal to stand around naked together while he played with my hair. Like it was just another average Sunday for us. And I liked it.

A lot.

He piled it on top of my head and began wrapping a rubber band—if the stretchy object ripping my neck hairs out was any indication—around it.

Once he'd knotted it into whatever semblance of a bun he'd been going for, he dropped his hands to my waist, sliding them down my sides and over my stomach.

"Your house is, um…" I swallowed. God, he was barely even touching me, I needed to get my shit together. "Well, it's so pristine and perfect. It just doesn't match the gruff, tattooed bartender vibe."

I winced, hoping that didn't come across as insulting as it sounded, but he only laughed, playfully swatting my ass, and stepped away.

"I think you'll find that my *vibe* is pretty fluid, Miss Lace."

He walked to the wall, and I watched him search through his collection of supplies, admiring every inch of him as he did. "So, are you going to tell me what we're doing in here?"

He grabbed, what looked like, a six-foot roll of paper propped against the shelf and dropped it to the tile. "I thought we'd end our night with a little fun."

My heart sank at his words, and my mind immediately leapt in front of it, waving a giant red flag and telling it to buck the fuck up. I'd known it would only be one night. That was the plan. Rebound with the hot, nameless bartender and go home. That was it.

I somehow managed to put a smile on my face and said, "I'm pretty sure we've already covered that."

He smirked, kicking the roll so it unraveled across the floor and covered the center of the room.

My heart rate picked up, wondering what in God's name he needed to cover the floor for. Strange man? Check. Lockable room? Check. Covering the floor for easy clean up? Comforting.

"What's that?"

"Heavyweight cotton canvas. Now get your ass over here before I lose my muse and fuck you against the wall."

The temptation to ask for option B was strong, but he looked so excited, and I was curious to see what exactly he wanted to do instead of sex.

I walked over, sashaying my hips and feeling a thrill when his cock twitched in answer. "So, what now, Mr. Muse? Are you going to draw me like one of your French girls?"

CHAPTER 12

Bartender

HER SMART MOUTH was going to be the death of my sanity. It made me want to abandon my plans, throw her over my lap, and spank her ass until it turned pink and hot beneath my hand. And only when she was drenched and screaming would I stop and take her from behind.

Fuck, there were so many things I wanted to do to her, and not even close to enough time. Every tick of the clock was a countdown to the night's inevitable end, and that'd been fine at first. Just another night and another lay.

Until I got a taste. The second I sank my tongue between her thighs and felt her explode on my face, it

changed.

I felt like I'd finally found religion. I wanted to worship at her altar, offer my tongue for her communion, and confess my sins while losing myself inside her. Hell, I wanted to fast for a week where the only thing I consumed was her.

And I didn't know what the hell to do about it. I felt lost. My hope was that if I fucked her hard enough and thoroughly enough, maybe it'd end this mental torment.

If I happened to create a permanent memento to remember her by in the process, so what? People had memorable one-night stands all the time. It didn't necessarily mean anything.

"No, Lacey-Lu," I said, answering her question. "I'm not going to draw you. I'm going to swirl paint all over this canvas, and then I'm going to spread you out and fuck you on it."

"That sounds...messy."

"My favorite way to have you." I wrapped my hands around the back of her neck, bringing her mouth to mine, and stole her reply. She immediately opened, slanting her mouth and letting me sweep in and take over.

I wanted to devastate this woman, making it impossible for her to ever forget me. I wanted to stain her skin, imprint the feel of my cock inside her body, and leave such a taste in her mouth that she'd be left comparing every new partner to me, only to come up short.

I wanted to ruin her.

"Tell me again, what you are," I whispered against her lips.

"Your whore."

Blood rushed through my veins at the complete ease with which she said the words, and my cock hardened in answer. "That's right. And as my whore, you're going to sit on the edge of the canvas and give me a show while I pour the paint."

She brushed her hands over my chest, leaning in to run the flat of her tongue across one of my nipples. "Am I allowed to finish?"

Goosebumps shot down my arms, and my tentative hold on my control began to fissure. "No. Not until I'm deep inside you. I just need you nice and ready for me, baby."

She looked down at the hard length of my cock, currently pressed between us, and bit her lip. I loosened my grip, letting her step away and lower to the ground.

My words had only been half the truth. I did need her wet and ready to take my size, but that wasn't the only reason. I also needed her on edge because I knew once I felt her clench around me, I wouldn't last long.

Not after everything we'd already done tonight. And I fucking refused to shoot my load before she did. I needed her to feel the same uncontrollable burning I was suffering from so we could erupt together.

Leaving her to get settled, I grabbed a container of alcohol-based paint from the shelf, filtering through my choices as I walked back. I'd do two colors. No, maybe a few varying shades of the two colors. Yeah, that'd be perfect.

"Pink and green, huh?" She breathed.

I set the container down and glanced her way. She was leaned back on one arm with her knees bent and the soles of her feet pressed together. The position spread her wide open, making her legs look like fucking butterfly wings.

She stared at me with heavy eyes, working her clit in slow, firm circles and I cracked a little further. I wanted to smack her hand away and replace it with my tongue, tasting her all over again.

"It suits us," I answered, knowing my voice sounded more like I was gurgling gravel than actual words. Without taking my eyes off her hand, I grabbed a few shades of each color, drizzling them sporadically over the canvas.

"Show me how you fuck yourself," I ordered, tossing the empty containers behind me and not caring if any got on the floor. I had tile for a reason.

She bit her lip, lying all the way down, and relaxed her thighs so they splayed out and exposed every inch of her. Fuck me. If I could choose what flashed before my eyes when I died, this would be it.

I watched, transfixed, as she slid two fingers up and down her cunt—effectively shredding my sanity—before finally pushing them in. Her free hand moved to one of her nipples, pulling and pinching while her other moved in steady, shallow thrusts.

"Tell me what you're imagining while you fuck yourself," I growled, tossing the last bottle and stepping toward her to better enjoy her show.

"You," she rasped, moving faster. "I'm imagining you inside me."

"Am I wearing a condom?"

Her head fell back, and she swallowed. "No. I—I'm on birth control."

"Thank fuck."

Not giving her time to process what I was doing, I wrapped my hands around her ankles and straightened her legs, dragging her across the canvas. A full belly laugh burst out of her when her body hit the colorful swirls, and my chest squeezed.

I ignored the unwelcome sensation, continuing to maneuver her until everything but her head was in paint. She shivered, but those deep blue eyes never lost their heat as she stared up at me.

Lowering to my knees, I straddled her, resting an elbow on either side of her head. "I can't wait any longer. Put me in, Lacey. Show me how bad this needy cunt wants me."

She moved with impressive speed, gripping my shaft and rubbing the weeping tip through her arousal. She was already so fucking wet, I was half-convinced being inside her was going to kill me.

She placed me at her entrance, rolling her hips to coax me in. When she couldn't get more than an inch due to my position, her lips pursed, and she looked seconds from combusting.

I chuckled, fucking living for her desperation. It fueled me, making my balls tighten with the need to explode inside her. Shifting my weight onto one arm, I wrapped my other around her neck, holding her in place, and pushed in another inch before pulling back out.

She cursed, clutching at my arm and leaving swirled handprints on my skin. "*Please.*"

"I do so love it when you beg."

Fighting the overwhelming urge to shove all the way, I clenched my jaw and continued easing into her, working a little farther with each push.

"You look so fucking good with me inside you," I said, pushing in a little harder. Her body tensed in answer, and she squeezed her eyes shut.

"Fuck, Bart, I don't know if I can—"

"You can take more." I leaned down to press my lips to hers, tightening my hold on her neck, and slammed the rest of the way in.

She cried into my mouth, instinctually trying to shift away, but I held her throat, pinning her in place for my use. Her pussy felt as fucking life changing as I knew it would. Hot, tight, and already trying to milk a release out of me.

"That's it, baby. Breathe."

She let out a string of curses and arched into me, wrapping her legs around my waist. Her paint-coated hands shot to my back as I began to move, and she dug her nails into my skin, trying in vain to stay quiet.

"Stop holding back, Lacey," I said, pulling out and shoving in to the hilt, again and again. "If the neighbors can't hear you, you're not fucking loud enough."

My knees were already screaming at me from pressing into the tile beneath the canvas, but I didn't stop. I continued rutting into her, moving my hand to her breast and rolling her nipple between my fingers.

Her back lurched off the ground, and she screamed, likely carving bloody nail marks into my skin.

"Yeah, that's it. Let everyone on this goddamn street know how much of a whore you are for me."

I was being a brute, but the demon inside just didn't fucking care. I felt wild and unhinged as I pulled away, gripping her waist and flipping her onto all fours.

I yanked her ass up, grabbing her hips and ramming back in. I could only imagine what my eyes looked like as I watched her hands claw at the canvas, slapping paint all over her arms.

"Fuck, look at you. Covered in paint and screaming out filth while a stranger's cock is buried in your cunt." I reached around her, finding her clit. "And you absolutely love it."

She cried out again, practically mewling into the canvas. I wanted to break her. Wanted her to scream 'ruby' if only to know, without a shadow of a doubt, she'd wince with every step she took tomorrow.

Every twirl she did on stage, every squat and twist and

shimmy, I wanted her to fucking feel the memory of me. Those customers might be allowed to look and want, but I'd fucking had her.

And goddamnit if I wasn't determined to leave a mark.

CHAPTER 13

Lacey

DEATH BY VIOLENT, cataclysmic railing. That's what my tombstone would read. That is, if I even had a body to bury after this.

Bart seemed intent on fucking me in half, and I was pretty sure I'd screamed, "no more" followed by "please" and "thank you" at least three times so far.

His fingers worked my clit harder, turning the heat coiled in my center into a raging inferno. I bucked against him, racing toward yet another release even as my body threatened to give out.

Sensing I was close, he steadied his pace, keeping his

thrusts deep, and focused his efforts on those goddamn fingers. 'Ruby' tickled at the back of my throat as the rhythm of unending stimulation had me half moaning and half weeping.

"Oh God, I can't…I can't."

"Give me one more, Lacey. I need to feel you clench around me. *Now*." He shoved into me as deep as he could go, pinching my clit as he did, and I detonated.

My vision went black, and my entire body turned into a live wire. I cried out, slapping at the wet canvas, and wishing he was in front of me so I could bite down on his shoulder or claw up his back. Something. Anything.

He groaned like he was in agony and shuddered as my inner muscles convulsed around him. He seemed to be struggling to hold back his own release, but he didn't move, continuing to circle that swollen bundle of nerves at the same pace until the last wave washed over me.

But the second my muscles went lax, and I heaved out a shaky breath of relief, he ripped himself away from me. It was so sudden, I didn't even have a chance to catch my breath before he was twisting me onto my back, shoving my legs up, and sinking back inside me.

His chest was flush against my paint-coated one, and his weight pressed me into the floor, but all I comprehended were his eyes. They were heated and serious as he rocked into me, over and over.

"This is how I always want to cum," he muttered, almost as if he were talking to himself, and then he captured my lips in a searing kiss.

I responded eagerly, cradling his head and sucking his tongue into my mouth. He trembled, gripping my shoulders and bucking into me erratically, chasing his climax.

I felt like a fucking goddess watching this man crumble at my touch, but I needed more. I needed *everything*. "Fucking fill me, Bartender."

His fingers dug into my skin hard enough to bruise, and he barked out a curse as he finally poured into me. I tightened my legs around him and rolled my hips under, taking as much of him as I could.

When he finished pumping the last drops inside me, he collapsed, dropping his forehead to rest on my shoulder. I couldn't help but smile, enjoying the heavy feel of his chest rising and falling against me. Circling my arms around him, I held him close, lightly running my nails down his spine.

"I don't know about you, Bart, but I could go again. I don't even think I broke a sweat," I said, choking back a laugh when his head rose to reveal a pair of narrowed eyes.

"That's because I did all the damn work," he said, pinching my side.

I squealed, twisting to escape, and the movement caused him to slip out of me. I winced at the sudden absence of him. I was going to be so fucking sore tomorrow.

Lowering my legs, I scrunched my nose when I felt his release seep out of me onto the canvas. "Oops."

He leaned back to sit on his heels, staring down

between us. "The animal in me wants to grab a plug and cork your cunt so it stays inside you, but the artist in me likes seeing our sex drip onto this."

"You're a little insane," I said, pushing up and running my hand over the wet, matted hair on the back of my head. So much for keeping my hair out of it.

"Why? People make souvenirs all the time. It's no different than a mother keeping a chunk of baby hair or making a milk ring."

I barked out a laugh, which only caused more to drip out of me. "A *what* ring?"

"You know, the jewelry mothers can get to put a drop of their breastmilk in. To remember the baby days and shit."

"Do I even want to know why you know that?"

He caressed his hands down my thighs, almost absentmindedly. "I've had partners in the past who were mothers. Some still actively breastfeeding," he said, wiggling his brows.

I laughed, giving him a look that said he'd lost his mind. "This is, by far, the weirdest post-sex conversation I've ever had."

He joined me, laughing and reaching up to flick me on the nose. "You say that now, but somehow I bet we'll have another even weirder."

He said it so naturally, like it was already decided that we'd do this again. It warmed me, and my heart leapt to my throat at the thought that maybe he felt the same way I did about what this was between us.

That it was more than just sex.

I smiled at him only for my poor, stupid heart to fall to my stomach when he didn't return it. Instead, he looked ten seconds from vomiting.

He swallowed, instantly pushing to his feet, and took a large step back. His hands shook, and he fisted them, staring down at his body. I followed his gaze, praying I was just imagining the tension radiating off him.

"Well, this is going to stain," I joked, pressing my hand over my hair again.

"That was kind of the point." He looked up and winked, but it held zero heat. "But if you shower now, you should be able to get the majority of it off before you leave. And it'll make for a fun story at work, I'm sure."

Turning away from me, he grabbed a stained rag from the container of supplies and began wiping his hands, like he was suddenly desperate to remove all evidence of tonight.

He glanced up when I didn't respond, and I tried to clear the hurt from my expression, but by the way he immediately looked away again, I was pretty sure I failed.

He moved the rag to his feet, scrubbing them almost angrily, and stepped off the canvas. "There's a bathroom across the hall you can use. Don't worry about staining the towels. I'm used to replacing them."

I flinched, his insinuation loud and clear. "Where are you going?"

"To shower as well. My bedroom and bathroom are off the kitchen on the main floor."

Feeling like a discarded toy abandoned on the floor, I pushed up to my feet as well, pressing my legs together and crossing my arms over my chest.

The comfort I'd felt walking naked with him earlier seemed like a joke, but maybe he was just trying to be nice and give me an out in case *I* wanted to leave. Maybe I just needed to let him know I didn't want to.

"We could just shower to—"

"Meet me downstairs when you're done, and I'll walk you back to your car," he said, the words coming out short and harsh. And with that, he spun, hightailing it out of the room like it was on fire.

I stared after him, feeling like I'd been slapped in the face. If there was an award for reading men incorrectly, I'd officially won it, hands down.

When would I learn that I didn't understand men at all? I went home with a guy I didn't even know the name of, thinking what? That he felt the same pull I did and would want to keep me?

He'd said exactly what he needed to, to get in my pants. Going on and on about "taking my power back" over Derek's hurtful words. And like a pathetic, dried-up sponge, I'd soaked that shit right up. I'd spread my legs, opened my mouth, and let a man spit on me and call me a whore because I'd believed him.

Hell, I *had* felt fucking powerful watching him come

undone above me. The irony was, *he'd* apparently never believed it.

I stared at the mess around me, noting the paint beneath my feet was now more brown than pink or green. It was practically a neon sign pinpointing exactly where our bodies had been on the canvas, and for whatever reason, it was my tipping point.

The tears that'd been stinging my eyes from the second he'd left, spilled over. I felt naïve and hurt and angry. At him, yes, but mostly at myself for letting him get to me. I needed to woman up and move on.

I'd probably watch a rom-com and eat a tub of ice cream first, but then I'd definitely move on.

I closed my eyes, taking a deep breath, and wiped my hands over my cheeks forgetting they were smeared with paint. Great.

If I wanted to keep any semblance of pride at my job, after already having the incident with Derek, I'd have to call out of my next shift until this shit faded.

There was no way I could walk into the club, in front of everyone I knew, wearing the stain of my poor life choices all over my body.

I glared at the doorway. You know what? No. Screw him. Screw men. I wasn't going to call out of work and lose money because I'd had good sex. That'd just fucking perpetuate the stigma I'd spent all night trying to shake off.

I was proud of who I was. It didn't matter what he, or anyone else, called me or thought about me. I'd liked tonight. I'd enjoyed every minute of it, including what he'd called me. And I was going to walk my tie-dyed ass in that club with my chin held high.

I refused to be ashamed.

I snatched the container of paint from where he'd left it next to the canvas and dug through it, smiling when I found what I was looking for.

Bart had, at least, been right about one thing.

Words did have power.

CHAPTER 14

Bartender

THE WATER WAS near scalding, and I let it cascade down my face, desperate to burn away the memory of her face. The way her smile had fallen and the subtle flinch of her eyes. It'd fucking gutted me.

I shouldn't have been such an ass and brushed her off like that. She deserved better, but I'd fucking panicked. Sitting in the middle of my studio, joking and laughing with her like we hadn't fucked like animals mere minutes prior, had felt too good. Too natural.

I'd smiled down at her, admiring the streaks and handprints all over us, and I could see it. A future, filled

with nights just like this one.

With her.

The unwelcome vision had caused me to speak without thinking. *I bet we'll have another even weirder.*

I'd said it like it was a given—a fact—that we'd do it again; the words spewing from my mouth before I could consider what they'd mean to her. What they meant to me.

A cold sweat had immediately shot down my spine, and I'd stared at her, horrified with the realization that I no longer had a desire to be with anyone else. I just wanted her.

No. Fuck. I didn't.

I grabbed my washcloth and scrubbed vigorously at my face, hoping the burn would snap me out of whatever spell she had me under.

Relationships weren't my thing. They never had been. Hell, I wouldn't even know where to begin with one. Lacey-Lu deserved so much better than that.

It'd been best to cut the whole thing off before any more damage was done. We'd accomplished what we'd set out to do, and that was that.

So what if I'd covered her in paint with the sole purpose of staining her skin before she returned to work. So what that I'd wanted—and *still* wanted—everyone to see it.

So what that I'd tried to be a gentleman and keep her hair clean, only to inevitably lose control and ruin it anyway with my need to feel more, have more, *take* more.

So. What.

It didn't mean anything.

I ground my teeth together, scrubbing at my body until it felt raw, but I couldn't get her out from where she'd burrowed under my skin. It'd only been ten minutes since I left, and I already wanted her again.

What did she look like soaking wet? Did her lips part when she tipped her head back and massaged her scalp? Did she still smell like me, or had all the evidence of our night already washed down the drain?

The thought had me gripping my cock and pumping it hard and fast, wishing it was her. If I got out now, I could catch her before she finished her own shower. I might even have time to grab anal beads and a bottle of lube on the way.

I could barge in and bend her over, working them into that perfect ass while I fucked her cunt from behind. Then we'd really see just how loud I could make her scream.

FUCK.

I released my dick, welcoming the way my balls ached as I denied myself release. I refused to get off to the image of her. Not when I could still fucking have her.

I twisted the water off, practically leaping out as I snatched a towel and ran it over my body. I needed to see her and figure out what this goddamn chaos in my mind meant.

Skipping boxers, I grabbed a pair of sweats from my dresser and worked them on, quickly stepping out of my room and into the kitchen.

I ran my fingers through my hair, combing the damp strands out of my face, and took a deep breath. I could do this. I just needed to see if what I felt was real. I needed to know what *she* thought this thing between us was.

I passed through the doorway leading to the living room, where'd I'd told her to be, only to find it empty and her clothes gone. I froze, staring at the spot they'd been, unable to move.

Maybe she'd just grabbed them before getting in the shower? That'd make sense. I listened, hoping beyond hope to hear the hum of water or the buzz of the bathroom fan, but the house was dead quiet.

"Lacey?"

More silence greeted me, and I felt my heart balloon up into my throat, cutting off my air supply and making me lightheaded. She didn't leave. After everything, there's no way she would've left without saying goodbye. Right?

Before I knew what I was doing, I was sprinting up the stairs, taking them two at a time. "Lacey!"

Nothing. I reached the landing, gasping for breath, to find both the bathroom and studio doors open and the rooms dark.

I ran down the hall, slamming my knuckles into the wall in my hurry to flip on the light. I already knew the truth, knew it deep down in my chest, but I still frantically searched for her anyway.

My studio was my life, showcasing my heart and soul in every piece I'd created. Every emotion and feeling was carved, etched, drawn, or painted into something tangible I could hold.

Yet the space had never felt more dead to me than it did the moment I realized the only thing I wanted to hold wasn't fucking there.

My chest hurt with how strong my heart beat against it, and I wondered if this was what a heart attack felt like.

I glanced to the center of the room where our painting sat, and fisted my hands at my sides, tempted to pour a bucket of white all over it. I very nearly did, until something on the canvas caught my eye.

Something that hadn't been there before.

Within a few long strides, I was standing over it, and what I saw stopped my heart entirely.

Right where our bodies had laid, she'd rubbed off as much paint as she could, using none other than her fucking lacy bodysuit, and stretched the ruined garment across the top.

And where the original paint had once been, were four words—four names—painted in big black letters. Each with a red 'X' slashed over them.

LACEY.

SLUT.

WHORE.

POWERLESS.

And right at the bottom, painted in red, was a fifth name. Her name.

Marissa.

CHAPTER 15

Bartender

HER REAL NAME hadn't even fully registered before I was out of the room, barreling down my stairs, and racing toward the front door.

I flung it open, hearing the hinges screech in protest as it bounced off the doorstop. Not even bothering to shut it, I launched myself onto the porch, blinking rapidly to acclimate to the darkness.

The night air whipped at my bare skin, and the debris on the cement dug into my feet, but it was all just white noise to the blood rushing in my ears. All I could think about was my desire to find her.

She'd left her car parked at the restaurant, so she'd either called a service to pick her up while I'd been in the shower, or she'd gone ahead and started walking. Praying she'd chosen the latter, I leapt off the porch, snapping my head to the left, and stared down the deserted street.

When my eyes latched on to absolutely nothing, I bowed my head, squeezing my eyes shut and digging my fingers into my hair. God, I was stupid.

So goddamn, fucking stupid.

I didn't have her last name or phone number. I didn't even know what club she worked at. And after the way I'd brushed her off, she'd never return to the restaurant and risk running into me. I'd never find her again, and the thought had me feeling hollow and frantic.

Maybe if I ran—

"Bart?"

My head whipped up at the name I never thought I'd want to hear so badly. I turned, my body already moving toward the sound of her voice before my eyes had even located her in the dark.

Marissa was perched on a row of cement blocks that bordered the small flower garden to the side of my porch. Tucked back as she was, she was hidden in the shadows, and I'd completely missed her in my hurry to check the street.

She looked a wreck. Her face was covered in streaks and smeared makeup, her hair was matted to her head, and her jacket and skirt did little to cover the paint she hadn't bothered to wash off.

She was the most beautiful thing I'd ever seen.

"What are you doing out here?" she asked, breaking our stare off to look down at the heels dangling from her fingers.

"Me? I was looking for *you*. You left."

"Yeah, that was kind of the plan, right?" She huffed out a short laugh like it didn't bother her, but I could see the dried tear trails on her cheeks. "It's late. I figured I'd just wash the night off in my own shower."

I cleared my throat, daring to take a step toward her. "Are you...waiting for someone?"

"No." She pushed off her thighs, standing and pulling her jacket tighter around her torso. "I was planning on walking back, but I haven't convinced myself to put my heels on yet. My feet didn't appreciate the walk to your place as it was."

I hadn't even thought about that when we'd left. Her toes had likely killed her the entire time. I cringed, wanting nothing more than to apologize and kiss each one.

"Don't."

She frowned, finally raising those blue eyes back on me. "Don't what? Put my shoes on?"

I dared another step. There was a good chance I'd already blown it and she'd have no interest in staying, but it was now or never. "Don't leave."

"You all but told me to."

"I know—shit, I know. I'm sorry."

She waved her hand, halting my confession. "Don't apologize, Bart. It's fine. I'm a big girl and can handle a quick walk of shame."

"It's not fine," I said, hating the way she was looking at me. "I don't want you to go."

She laughed, the sound having a bitter edge to it. "You're just saying that because you feel bad. And I told you, it's fine. I knew what tonight was."

"Really? Because I sure as hell don't anymore. All I can think about is taking you back inside. I want to rub your feet and shit and fall asleep with you cradled against me."

Her eyes widened, the fire in them sizzling out to embers at the truth I ripped from my heart and laid at her feet.

"Look, Bart, if you're just wanting—"

"*You*," I snapped, the word coming out like a curse. "You. Not one time and not one night. Fuck, Marissa, I can count on one hand the things I know about you, yet I want you so badly, I feel like I'm losing my mind. I don't fucking understand it."

She relaxed her grip on her jacket and dropped her heels to the ground, moving to stand closer to me. "I see you got my message."

Taking her nearness as a positive sign, I crossed the last foot of space between us and took her face in my hands, tipping her head back, and drinking her in.

"I need you to cure this insanity I feel. Because I don't know what to do if you don't." I brushed my thumbs across her cheeks, inhaling the lingering remnant of her perfume. It smelled like fucking *home*.

"I like sex, Marissa. I've always liked sex. Male, female,

single, group, you name it. But now, the thought of even touching someone other than you makes me want to peel my skin off. The feeling scared me. It still scares me."

"So, is that all you want me for then? To touch? Just friends with benefits until you've had your fill?"

"Yes. No. I mean, yes, I want your body, but that's not all I want. I just—" I dropped my head and rested my forehead against hers.

"I can't promise to do any of this right, and I can't promise this will work out. There's a high chance you'll get sick of my shit and leave before we ever become anything official."

She smirked, wrapping her arms around my waist. "Probably."

"What I *can* promise you, Marissa, is that I will give, whatever this is, my all while we try." I leaned down slowly, giving her every chance to pull away, but she only lifted onto her toes and pressed her lips to mine.

I gripped her face harder, holding her to me, and ran the tip of my tongue across her lips. She responded, opening her mouth and accepting everything I gave her.

She took it all, and only when we were both gasping for air, did I force myself to pull away. She tilted her head, staring up at me, and quirked her lips to the side.

"What?" I asked, soaking in the feeling of her hands on my skin.

She smiled wide, and I swore it lit up the night sky. "You can call me Mari."

I struggled to form words when all my mouth wanted to do was kiss that fucking smile. "You sure? I can think of a few other names I enjoyed calling you. They're graffitied upstairs if you need a reminder."

She laughed, leaning her head into my palm. "I think I'd prefer a different type of reminder."

"Yeah?" I hovered my mouth over hers again, sliding my hands to cup her ass and pull her against me. "In that case, it's nice to meet you, Mari. I'm Nate. Why don't you come inside, you look like you could use a really long shower."

Also by Lilian T. James

Meet Nate's friend, Curly

Madison gave her heart to a boy at the age of sixteen, but all she got in return was a broken heart and a swollen belly.

Alone with a baby and desperate for the love she hadn't found, she turned to a man who sealed his claim of devotion with a diamond ring.

He promised her a family. A life. A future. But his lies had only been a cover for the personal hell he introduced her to daily.

Now, at twenty-five, Madison has long since stopped believing in love. Balancing single parenthood, three jobs, and online courses, she doesn't have the time anyway.

So when the broody neighbor living in the other side of her duplex leaves a rude note on her door, she's not interested.

Not in his dark hair, not in his physique, and definitely not in the dimples she's only seen a hint of. She's one hundred percent, absolutely, not interested.

Not even a little.

Acknowledgements

First, I want to thank the individual who Nate's character was loosely crafted from. Thank you for every painting you've ever made me and for being my friend for the last two decades, even when we go years in-between seeing each other.

I will never forget the late-night phone calls in middle school to talk about dreams or how we once painted our lips so we could "mark" your wall before we painted it.

Next, I want to thank my editor, Elaine, who didn't bat an eye when I told her I had 20,000 words of smut for her to work through. You're a trooper, and I appreciate everything you've done for each book.

Lastly, I want to thank every one of my readers. It was because of all of you that this story even came to be. Nate had been one of my favorite characters in *Meet Me Halfway*, but I'd had no plan to write a story for him any time soon.

However, as soon as reviews began coming in for *Meet Me Halfway*, and you all started talking about sequels and spice, this story immediately came to life.

It *demanded* to be written.

I am so incredibly lucky to have the family, friends, and readers that I do. I love you all.

About the Author

Lilian T. James was born and raised in a small town of Kansas until she finished high school. Enrolling at a University on the east coast, she moved there with her son and obtained degrees in Criminal Justice, Social Work, Psychology, and Sociology. After graduating, she met her husband and moved to the west coast for a few years before they finally settled back in Kansas. She has three kids, one miniature dachshund, and has been an avid fantasy and romance reader her entire life. Lilian was finally able to publish her first novel, *Untainted*, in 2021 and has no plans of stopping.

Printed in the USA
CPSIA information can be obtained
at www.ICGtesting.com
LVHW030211160524
780459LV00030B/528

9 781737 889977